BUTTERFINGERS

Dennis Reader

Houghton Mifflin Company
Boston   1991

Benjamin Butters was known to everybody as Butterfingers.
He was always dropping things.

"It's as if his fingers were covered in butter,"
said Mrs. Butters.
"Or margarine," said Mr. Butters.

Benjamin dropped his toast butter-side down,
usually on the dog...

and the pet goldfish on the cat.

All of this was a great worry to Mrs. Butters, who was soon expecting another baby.

Mr. Butters said he'd have his work cut out worrying
about the new baby, so Benjamin should stay with
his grandparents for a while.

Grandad and Grandma Butters lived on a small farm
that smelled of pigs and cows and chickens because
that's what they kept and it was super.

Grandad Butters once let Benjamin collect the eggs.
Afterwards Grandad Butters said once was enough.

Grandma Butters said Benjamin could feed Pauline the pig.
"After all," she said, "you can't slop slops!"

But Benjamin could...

And after Druscilla the cow gave her best bucket
of milk in a lifetime...

Benjamin somehow tipped it all over the duck.

So, if you were able to ask...

the Butters' dog...

the Butters' cat...

any chicken...

the Butters' goldfish...

the duck...

Pauline the pig...

...or Druscilla the cow if Benjamin was a bit of a butterfingers they would be inclined to agree.

One day Grandma Butters took a phone call that
made her very happy.
"You've got a new baby sister," she told Benjamin.
"You can soon go home."

Benjamin wasn't sure if the news of her granddaughter
had made Grandma happy or if it was because he
was going home.

Anyway he tried not to drop too many things before he left.

When Benjamin and Grandad and Grandma arrived there were uncles and aunts Benjamin couldn't remember ever having seen before...

...and they were all making strange noises and poking their fingers at the baby, who wiggled her toes and seemed to quite enjoy it.

"Come and meet your new baby sister," said Benjamin's mom.

She was almost as pink as the baby and looked very happy.

Benjamin looked closely at the baby.   She had eyes like
screwed-up blackcurrants.
"Can I hold her?" he asked his mom.

Benjamin's dad went rigid in a kind of way...the uncles and aunts and grandparents seemed to stop breathing as Benjamin's mom said, "Of course you can... but be careful..."

Benjamin tucked his arms under the baby and held her
to him. She was woolly warm. Her fingers gripped
tight around his. And then she smiled at him.

It was a wonderful smile.

Baby Butters knew she was safe.
Benjamin wasn't going to drop her.

She was his sister.